152690

repl

War of the Clones

MARILYN KAYE

BANTAM BOOKS
NEW YORK • TORONTO • LONDON • SYDNEY • AUCKLAND

RL 5.5, 008–012

WAR OF THE CLONES

A Bantam Skylark Book / October 2002

ISBN 0-553-48767-1

Visit us on the Web! www.randomhouse.com/kids

Published simultaneously in the United States and Canada

Bantam Skylark is an imprint of Random House Children's Books, a division of
Random House, Inc. SKYLARK BOOK and colophon and BANTAM BOOKS
and colophon are registered trademarks of Random House, Inc. Bantam Books,
1540 Broadway, New York, New York 10036.

PRINTED IN THE UNITED STATES OF AMERICA

OPM   10   9   8   7   6   5   4   3   2   1

For Manuel Vilaret, Rosa Sanchez, Pablo, and Alex

War of the Clones

one

When Amy opened the front door to her best friend, she could see that Tasha was bursting with news.

"Have you seen this?" Tasha Morgan asked, waving a newspaper in the air.

Amy recognized the infamous tabloid and groaned. "No, I don't read the *Universal Reporter,* and neither should you. It's worse than the *National Enquirer!*"

Tasha drew herself up haughtily. "For your information, Amy Candler, *I* don't normally read the *Universal Reporter* either. But I was standing in the checkout line at the supermarket when I saw this headline and thought

I'd make an exception." Dramatically, she held the front page up to Amy's face. In letters twice as big as those found in any respectable newspaper, the headline blared, MASTER RACE CREATED ON ISLAND PARADISE.

Using her speed-reading skills, Amy absorbed the entire article in slightly more than three seconds. Which was good, since it wasn't worth any more time than that.

The article was highly sensationalized, of course. According to the *Universal Reporter,* there was an island in the Pacific Ocean where mad scientists were hard at work developing a colony of superhumans. Their plan was to use this new, powerful generation to take over the world. What the story lacked in details it made up for in exclamation points.

"Garbage," Amy declared.

"Of course it's garbage," Tasha agreed. "But the description of the island sounds just like that place where you went."

Amy shrugged and tossed the newspaper onto the coffee table. "I'm starving."

Happily, Tasha agreed with that statement too. "I'll order the pizzas. What do you want for toppings?"

"Anything except onions and anchovies."

Tasha went into the kitchen, and Amy found her

eyes straying to the coffee table. Quickly, she read the front-page story again.

She had to admit that Tasha was right. The island described in the article sounded exactly like the island where Amy had spent a very strange week less than a year ago. But this description would probably fit a million places. Didn't all island paradises have sunshine, exotic flowers, palm trees swaying in the breeze, stuff like that? *Hers* certainly had. In all honesty, it had been a beautiful place—although Amy's trip hadn't exactly been a tropical vacation.

Tasha called to her from the kitchen. "Who's going to be here? How many pizzas should I get?"

Amy made a list out loud. "You, me, Eric, Chris, Andy. Mom's working late, so we're five. Get two large."

Andy Denker had been on the island with her. All Project Crescent clones had been brought there, mostly against their will. They'd been tested for various behavior. . . .

Tasha's voice broke into the ugly memory. "Should I get those twisty curly cheesy things? They're only a dollar more."

"Okay." Amy was still looking at the article. She had practically committed it to memory by now. What will Andy say about it? she wondered. Surely he'd agree with her that it was nonsense. After all, just about everyone had escaped from the island.

Not all of them, though. How many had remained behind? She knew about the seven clones who had been through the treatment that wiped out emotions by waking a dormant gene. And then there was that awful Annie Perrault, who was so nasty she hadn't even needed a treatment. Four Amys, four Andys. Was that enough to create a master race?

With determination, Amy pushed the thought out of her head. This was the *Universal Reporter,* for crying out loud! It didn't deserve her attention.

Tasha returned. "I ordered *three* pizzas," she told Amy. "You know how my brother can eat."

Amy nodded. "Yeah, that was probably smart. Chris and Andy can put it away too. They've been eating over here a lot lately."

The two boys had been back in Los Angeles for two weeks, and they were currently living in the condo on the other side of the Morgans. Amy's neighbor, Monica Jackson, was off on a two-week meditation retreat in Nepal, and she'd been pleased to give her place to the boys temporarily in exchange for getting her plants watered, her cats fed, and her mail collected. Since neither of them really had a home or a family, Andy and Chris had gladly taken her up on her offer.

"How come they're eating over here?" Tasha asked. "Doesn't Monica's place have a kitchen?"

"Of course it has a kitchen. But neither of them can cook."

Tasha rolled her eyes. "That's no excuse. All Andy would have to do is read a cookbook and he could be a professional chef. So could you, for that matter."

"Probably," Amy acknowledged. With her altered and enhanced genetic makeup, she could learn to do anything quickly, and Andy had the same capabilities.

"So why aren't we having a gourmet dinner tonight instead of pizza?"

Amy shrugged. "I can't do *everything*."

"Sure you can," Tasha stated.

Amy grinned. "Okay, I *can*. I just don't want to. If I did it once, people would expect me to cook for them all the time."

Tasha understood. "I guess genetic superiority doesn't make you any less lazy than me."

"Exactly," Amy said. But just to show off the difference between them, she said, "Andy and Chris are here."

There hadn't yet been a knock on the door, but Amy's

supersensitive hearing had picked up the sound of footsteps getting closer. Of course, she couldn't swear the visitors would be Andy and Chris. Her abilities didn't include seeing through walls, and she wasn't psychic. But it was a good guess, and she was right.

"Hi, guys," she greeted them as she opened the front door. "What's up?"

"Not much," Andy said.

"You seen this?" Chris Skinner asked. He was carrying a newspaper.

Andy groaned. "Chris, I told you, it's garbage."

"Is that the *Universal Reporter*?" Tasha asked.

"No, it's something called the *World Examiner*," Chris replied. "They're running a series about cloning."

"Yeah, along with the latest reports on UFO and Elvis sightings," Andy said.

"Let me see that," Amy said. The *World Examiner* was another supermarket tabloid, but it was a little more respectable than the *Universal Reporter*. She read part three of the series the paper was calling A NEW HUMAN RACE.

It was vague, just like the story in the *Universal Reporter*, but there were several more details in this article. It referred to a secret organization and experiments in human cloning that had begun seventeen years ago.

The cloned beings had a human genetic source, it said, but then their genes had been altered and advanced to make the clones as close to humanly perfect as possible. Twelve males had been followed three years later by twelve females. And now that the clones were ready to mate . . .

"*You're* not ready to mate," Tasha declared. She'd been reading the article over Amy's shoulder.

"Not emotionally," Amy murmured. "But physically . . ."

"Are the pizzas here yet?" Andy demanded.

Amy didn't answer him. "Andy, they've got the dates and numbers right."

"Coincidence," Andy declared. "They don't mention Project Crescent by name, and they don't know about the new acceleration process." That was something Chris had discovered at the organization's headquarters in Washington, D.C. Scientists had developed a means to accelerate the clones' growth hormones so that they could age more rapidly and generations of perfect people could be produced practically overnight.

The newspapers clearly didn't know everything. Even so . . . "This is creepy," Amy said. "There was something in the *Universal Reporter,* too, about clones on an island."

Andy took the newspaper away from her. "Amy, if something like this was really going on, we'd know about it already. Mr. Devon would have contacted us."

His patronizing tone was annoying. "Well, I still think we should come up with a plan of action," Amy declared.

Andy grinned. "The only plan I'm interested in right now is the plan for dinner." He cocked his head to one side. "Someone's coming. I hope it's the pizza guy."

It wasn't. Eric Morgan, Tasha's brother, was the next arrival. But the pizzas arrived soon after. Amy gathered plates, Tasha put some music on, and everyone gathered around the dining room table. For a while there was no more talk of cloning.

Amy was still thinking about it, though. When two tabloids reported on the same nonsense, maybe it *wasn't* nonsense—at least not all of it. She and Andy couldn't sit around and do nothing. If the organization's goals were in the process of being achieved, they had to get involved. She needed to convince him that they should take action.

But clearly not tonight. Everyone was relaxed and in a good mood. School was out for spring break, and the topics of discussion were beaches and picnics, not master-race conspiracies. Amy tried to join the conversation. It wasn't until later, when everyone had left, that she took the newspapers up to her room and read the articles again.

She'd just finished when she heard the front door open downstairs. "Honey, I'm home," her mother called.

Hastily, Amy shoved the newspapers under her mattress. There was no point in upsetting her mother until she found out more. "There's leftover pizza in the fridge," she called back.

Nancy Candler appeared at her doorway. "Thanks, but I'm too tired to eat. I think I'll go right to bed."

Amy blew her a kiss. " 'Night, Mom." As soon as her mother disappeared, Amy took a pad of paper out of her desk drawer and started thinking about a plan.

#1, she scrawled at the top of the paper. *Find Mr. Devon.*

She had no idea where to find him, the man who had always provided her with inside information about the organization. But she had several phone numbers and e-mail addresses. And she'd ask Andy, since he was the last to see Mr. Devon.

#2, she wrote. *Contact Amys.*

Not all of them, of course. She didn't even know

how to reach most of her sister clones. But she had an e-mail address for Amy Sherman, Number Eight, who lived in New York. She also had a phone number for Aly Kendricks, but she wasn't sure she'd call. Aly was the thirteenth clone, the only one whose genes hadn't been successfully altered. In the past, Aly had posed as Amy, Number Three, who died, but Aly had no real powers. Still, she might know how to reach some of the others. . . .

The phone in her bedroom rang, and Amy snatched it up before the noise could wake her mother. "Hello?"

"It's me," Andy said. His voice was tense. "Have you checked your e-mail?"

"Not since this morning," Amy said. "Why?"

"Look at it now."

Amy opened the file and ran a mail download. There was one new message, from an unknown sender. She clicked on it.

The message had been sent to twenty-four mailboxes. It was brief and to the point.

There have been alarming developments in Project Crescent. We must take action. I am calling for all Amys and Andys to meet with me this Thursday at 2:00.

Amy recognized the name of a town on the southern California coast, not too far from San Diego, and the address given was for the town's public library. The message was signed *Amy 5*.

She remembered Amy, Number Five, very well. When they'd first met, at a hospital in New York, she'd discovered that Five was aligned with the organization. But then on the island, Five had revealed herself to be a double agent, only pretending to be working with the organization people in order to fight them.

"I think we should go to this meeting," Andy said.

Amy was taken aback. "So you're willing to believe *her* when you wouldn't listen to me."

"Well, Amy Five struck me as being pretty savvy," Andy said.

Amy bristled. "Like *I'm* stupid?"

Andy sighed. "Look, I'm just saying that now I think maybe there *is* something going on. So do you want to go or not?"

Amy found it irritating that Andy was so quick to respond to someone else's plea when he'd essentially ignored her own concerns. Personally, she doubted that Amy Five had any inside info.

But if something was happening, or was about to happen, she definitely wanted to be in on it. "Yeah, okay. Let's go."

two

Amy was *not* in a good mood. First of all, she had lied to her mother that morning, which she'd done before but which always made her feel crummy. Second, it was a gorgeous day and she was stuck inside a bus for almost five hours. Finally, she'd come to realize that her superhealthy constitution did not make her immune to some mild motion sickness.

"This better be worth the effort," she muttered.

Andy looked up from his book. "What?"

"I said, I hope this trip isn't a total waste of time."

"I doubt it," Andy said. "That e-mail seemed pretty

urgent. I think Amy Five must be on to something." He started reading again.

Amy wasn't convinced. "Maybe you just trust her because she has the same number *you* have. Andy Five and Amy Five. You sound like a team."

Andy looked up again. "What?"

Amy sighed. "Never mind." And he went back to his book. How can he read on this bus? Amy wondered. The mere thought of reading made her nauseous. Of course, it was probably psychological, but what difference did that make? The best she could do for entertainment was to keep her Walkman headset clamped to her ears. She hoped the batteries wouldn't run out, because she hadn't brought any extras. She'd had no idea the trip would take *this* long, what with all the traffic and the stops to pick up and drop off passengers.

Thank goodness she'd told her mother that the horror-movie marathon was a full-day event. Of course, her mother had wanted to know why she was going to spend a beautiful day like this cooped up in a movie theater. Amy had been forced to play the typical moody teenager—she'd just shrugged and said she felt like it, and her mother had bought the lie.

Andy opened his backpack and pulled out a bag of trail mix. "Want some?" he asked.

"No thanks." Amy wasn't crazy about the mixture of nuts and raisins, especially since she still felt a little nauseous. Suddenly Andy noticed her necklace for the first time.

"Why are you wearing *that*?" he asked.

Amy fingered the horse teeth that were strung on a leather cord. It had belonged to Lulu, a girl she had met under unusual circumstances. Usually it hung on the mirror in her bedroom.

In answer to Andy's question, she shrugged. "I think it looks cool."

He responded by rolling his eyes, which jerked her bad mood up a notch. "You're showing off," he announced.

She bristled. "What do you mean?"

"You want the other clones to ask about it so you can tell them how you went back in time to the Stone Age."

"That's ridiculous," Amy declared. But Andy wore a know-it-all smile as he offered her trail mix again.

"You want them all to know you've had more exciting adventures and experiences than they've had," he continued. "You want to be the big shot."

Amy glared at him. "That is *so* not true!"

"I understand how you feel," Andy went on. "It's not easy being one of twelve. It can get competitive. You want to establish your own identity."

Amy looked suspiciously at the title of the book he was reading. It was *Inside the Mind of the Multiple-Birth Teenager*. That figured. "So now you think you're a psychologist, huh?"

"Look, all I'm saying is it's normal to feel that way. But you have to remember that the other clones have probably had interesting experiences too. They might have something to tell *you*. Us," he amended quickly.

"I know that!"

"Good. Because you don't want to come across as if you think you're superior to the other Amys and Andys. Whatever's going on, we need to be united and work together."

"I *know*," Amy snapped. "You don't have to lecture me."

"I'm not lecturing you, I'm reminding you."

"Well, you don't need to remind me either!" She increased the volume on her Walkman and slumped back in her seat.

They barely spoke again until they got off the bus.

Looking around the small station, Amy didn't see any schedules posted. "I'm going to find out what time we need to be here to get back to L.A.," she said.

"I'll go ask," he offered. "And then we'll get some lunch. We have an hour before the meeting starts."

He was trying to make up for being so obnoxious earlier, and Amy knew she'd end up forgiving him—but maybe not as quickly as she thought she would. Because when he returned from the information counter, he had bad news.

"There's no bus back tonight."

"*What?*"

"The next bus leaves tomorrow morning at eight."

"Oh, that's just great," Amy fumed. "Thanks a lot, Andy. Now I have to call my mother and tell her the truth and get grounded for the rest of my life. Why didn't you find this out before?" Even as she said that, she knew it would have been just as easy for *her* to call and get the bus schedule. But Andy was the one who was so fired up about coming to this stupid meeting instead of waiting for Amy to come up with a better plan.

At Taco Bell, they stood in line for ages and had ten minutes to actually eat. By the time they arrived at the address Amy Five had given them, Amy's tolerance level had sunk to an all-time low. She was in no mood to be friendly to the other clones.

"Put on your sunglasses," she instructed Andy. It had been *her* idea to wear sunglasses, and she'd sent that message out to everyone Amy Five had contacted. If the clones didn't make some attempt to cover their features, people in the library would freak out when they saw a crowd of identical teens. Amy couldn't help feeling a little smug about the fact that Amy Five hadn't thought of that.

As it turned out, Amy didn't have to worry about a crowd. Only four others were in the library—three Amys, one Andy. Still, Amy felt unnerved, as she always did when she saw her own face again and again. Changes in hair style and color made it impossible for her to recognize and identify any of the clones, so they all had to reintroduce themselves.

"Hi, I'm Amy, Number Five," a girl in khaki capris and a light-green twinset said.

"I'm Seven," Amy said. "This is Andy Five."

"That's One and Eight," Five said, indicating the other two Amys. "And he's Andy Eleven."

"Hi," everyone chorused. Amy felt a nasty pleasure in seeing that Amy Five had only been able to round up this small group. Six out of a possible twenty-four—twenty-five, counting Aly—wasn't much of a turnout. She didn't notice the figure sitting in the shadow by the door until Five introduced him.

"And I guess you guys know Mr. Devon."

three 3

Amy was surprised. She had no idea that Five had been able to contact Mr. Devon. But was this the *real* Mr. Devon? He could be one of the many Devon androids. And back on the island, there had been Devon clones, too.

But when this Devon made eye contact with her and gave her a faint smile, Amy felt reasonably sure that he was for real. And when he spoke, she felt even more reassured. Devon androids didn't speak at all, and she'd never seen a Devon clone smile.

Real Mr. Devon didn't smile for long, though. He became very serious as he addressed the small group.

"I wish there were more of you here," he said. "I have no idea as to the size of the army the organization has built up on the island. And I don't know whether you'll want to challenge them. I think you *should*, but there is a risk involved. This has to be your decision."

"It could be dangerous," Amy Five told them. "Most of the clones didn't respond to my e-mail. Maybe they don't want to get involved, or maybe they're already on the island. They could have been treated, like the ones who stayed behind, so that they're aligned with the organization."

Amy's eyes darted back and forth from Amy Five to Mr. Devon. She was puzzled. Had they been planning this together? Why had Mr. Devon contacted Five instead of her?

Amy One clutched the hand of Andy Eleven and looked frightened. "What do they want to do to us?"

Five spoke patiently. "What they've always wanted to do. Use us to create a master race. They want us to get it started. They want the Amys and Andys to, you know, get together. Make babies."

One was less frightened now, and she glanced coyly at Eleven. "I wouldn't mind *that*," she said.

Amy remembered that One and Eleven had been a couple back at the island. Apparently they still were. But what was more interesting to her—and more annoying as well—was the way Five was acting like a know-it-all. It was time for Amy to show that she too possessed very important information.

"The organization has developed another treatment," she announced. "They can speed up the aging process. That allows them to create an entire generation in less than a week." She was about to add that they'd experimented on *her*, aging her ten years overnight, when Five broke in.

"Yes, they can age us ten years overnight," Five said. "They may have already begun doing this to the clones on the island. We can't afford to waste any time, we have to stop them *now*. Are you all with me?"

Amy's mouth dropped open. With *her*? Who put Five in charge? It was even more irritating to see Mr. Devon nod in agreement. When did the two of them get so chummy? Amy always thought Mr. Devon was closest with *her*, Number Seven.

One, Eight, and Andy Eleven were bobbing their heads, acknowledging Five's leadership. Her own Andy was nodding too. No one seemed to notice that Seven was less than enthusiastic.

"There's a boat waiting at the marina," Mr. Devon told them. "It's already stocked with supplies. Food, toothbrushes, all that."

"Lip gloss?" Eight asked. "Sunscreen?"

"Everything we need," Five told her.

So now everyone seemed to be in agreement: they had to go back to the island and stop the organization. Even Amy had to admit that it was the right thing to do. She just wished *she'd* been the one to propose it.

They all put their sunglasses back on and headed out of the library, Mr. Devon and Five in the lead. Andy hurried on ahead to speak quietly to Mr. Devon about something. One and Andy Eleven were hand in hand, whispering. Which left Amy trailing behind with Eight.

"I can't believe you came all the way from New York," Amy said to her.

"Why wouldn't I?" Eight challenged her.

Amy remembered that Amy Sherman had an aggressive manner, and she didn't let the girl's attitude put her off. In their past encounters, they'd had a good rapport.

"I'm just surprised, that's all," Amy said. "That's a long trip to make just because Five said we should have a meeting. Did you fly? That must have been expensive."

Eight shrugged, thrust her hands in her jeans pockets, and quickened her pace so she wasn't side by side with Amy. Clearly she wasn't in the mood to talk.

At the town marina, the boat was waiting for them. It was white with blue trim, very ordinary-looking, with the name *Bluefish* scrawled in blue paint on one side. A plank had been set up on the wharf for them to walk onto the boat.

Just as Amy, the last of the group, crossed the plank, she heard a high-pitched call from way behind her. "Wait! Wait for me!" She turned to see another Amy running toward them. It took a while for the girl to catch up because she was running at a normal pace—but of course, she had to since there were other people around, and running at clone speed would have drawn attention to the group.

She arrived, pretending to be breathless, and Amy Five took over again. Mr. Devon seemed to have disappeared.

"We'll be pushing off in just a minute," Five said. "If you want to call home, do it now, before we're out of range." She pulled a mobile phone from her sack, and Amy One was the first to take it. Amy watched and listened, curious to hear what One would tell her family as an excuse.

"Hi, Sarah, it's me. Tell Mom and Dad that Andy and I went on a camping trip with his uncle, okay? I'll call when I can. Bye."

How easy it was for her, Amy marveled. Sarah, whoever she was—a sister, probably—would be the one to get hassled by their parents for not getting a more complete message. Amy One then offered the phone to Andy Eleven, who left a similar message, only this time he and One were camping with *One's* uncle. Andy didn't need to use the phone—he had no one to call. Nor, apparently, did Eight.

"I blew my parents off," she announced in a rough voice. "I'm on my own now."

The new girl didn't need to use the phone either, so it was Amy's turn. There was a sickening feeling in the pit of her stomach as she hit the buttons. She didn't know what kind of story she'd be able to come up with.

Lucky for her, she got the answering machine. "Mom, I'm going to be away for a few days. Don't worry, I'm with Andy, and Mr. Devon is here too. I'll call when I can." And she hung up. This message was not going to satisfy Nancy Candler, but it was better than Amy disappearing with no word at all.

The plank was taken away and the anchor lifted, and the *Bluefish* pulled away from the wharf. The others went down to check out the sleeping quarters, and Amy went in search of Mr. Devon. She found him at the helm, steering the boat out to sea.

"What's going on?" she asked him. "I mean *really*. I'll bet you know more than you're saying. You can tell me."

But Mr. Devon didn't appear to be in the mood to tell anyone anything. He didn't even look in her direction.

Amy couldn't help it—she was hurt. "I don't get it. How come you talked to Five?"

"He can't answer you."

Amy turned to find herself facing Five. "Why not?"

"Because he's not Mr. Devon. He's an android."

Amy gasped. "So you *are* working for the organization! You and this android are turning us over to them!"

"Don't be silly," Five said. "That was the real Mr. Devon at the library. He went on ahead by helicopter. These androids don't have any loyalties. This one's working for us."

Amy was skeptical. "The last Amy to arrive—how did she know where to find us?"

Five explained. "Mr. Devon left word with the librarian, in case anyone asked for us. Honestly, Seven, there's no conspiracy or secret agenda going on here. We're all on the same side."

The latest arrival appeared on deck. "It's cool down there!" she bubbled. "The bunk beds are really comfortable. And there are the cutest little toiletry kits for each of us, with little-bitty soaps and toothpaste and even bath gel!"

Amy eyed her suspiciously. There was a strangely familiar quality about her, and it wasn't just the fact that she looked exactly like all the others. Then Amy noticed something quite different about her, and she drew in her breath sharply.

"Are those *real* pierced earrings?" she asked, pointing to the gold hoops on the new girl's ears.

"Of course they're real!" the girl replied. "I would never wear those stick-on kind, they're for wimps who are afraid of getting their ears pierced."

Amy glared at her grimly. "Or for Project Crescent clones who lose all their powers when their earlobes are pierced!"

The girl's mouth fell open, and she looked at Five in consternation. "Really?"

Five sighed. "It doesn't matter for you, Aly. You don't have any powers."

"Aly!" Now Amy was completely blown away. "You're Aly Kendricks? The thirteenth clone?"

Aly nodded ruefully. "Yeah, it's me, the dud. Hi, Amy. I guess I should call you Seven here."

Normally Amy would have been happy to see her old friend. But she was furious, and mainly at Five. "Why did you invite her? It isn't safe! She can't protect herself the way we can!"

"I know she's not exactly like us," Five said. "But she's still one of us. And she's smart. She came through on the island before, remember?"

"Of course I remember," Amy snapped. Back on the island, Aly had taken on the role of Amy, Number Three, a clone who had died in a hospital experiment two years before. "But this time it's different. It's even more dangerous!"

"It was my decision," Aly declared hotly. "I know the risks."

Amy ignored her and directed her fury at Five. "You shouldn't have told her about this!"

Their raised voices had drawn Eleven, One, Eight, and Andy onto the deck. "What's going on?" Andy asked.

Amy pointed an accusing finger at Five. "She invited

Aly Kendricks to join the battle. Aly isn't genetically advanced—she can't defend herself!"

"I can too!" Aly yelled. "In my own way!"

Five managed to keep her voice calm and neutral. "Maybe I was wrong. It's not too late to turn the boat back to shore and leave Aly behind. Let's vote on this. All in favor of letting Aly stay, raise your hand."

Amy watched in dismay as all other hands went up, including Andy's. At least he had the decency to give her an apologetic face as he did it.

"All opposed?"

Amy was alone. She pressed her lips together tightly and walked across the deck to the stairs. Before she descended, she looked back and spoke. "If anything happens to Aly, it's all your fault!"

The words sounded childish, even to her own ears. As she went downstairs, she knew this wasn't the right way to behave—if she really wanted to take the leadership role away from Five.

four

Dinner was in boxes distributed by the silent Devon android. Each of the clones received a chicken sandwich, pasta salad in a plastic cup, a bag of chips, an apple, and a chocolate bar with almonds. Amy took her box and sidled over to Eight, who was alone sitting on a deck chair.

"What do you want?" Eight asked rudely.

Again Amy was a little startled. Eight had never sounded so tough before. "I just want to talk," she said.

Eight eyed her with suspicion. "About what?"

Amy considered her options. She remembered that

Eight was a no-nonsense person, not someone to dance around. "About Amy Five. She's acting awfully bossy, don't you think? Like who died and left *her* in charge?"

"I don't know," Eight replied.

"Well, I didn't mean that *literally*," Amy added. Eight's forehead puckered, as if she didn't know what the word *literally* meant. Amy elaborated. "You see how she's giving directions and making decisions. How come it's not . . . well, one of us?"

Eight shrugged. "Who cares?"

"*I* care!" Amy said indignantly. "You should too."

The only response she got was another shrug. Amy frowned. Clearly she had to approach this relationship with Eight from another direction. She looked around for a subject and noticed the backpack by Eight's feet.

"What's in there?"

Eight actually answered. "Weapons."

"Weapons? What kind of weapons?"

"The usual stuff. Bombs, explosives. Dynamite. Better not get too close."

Amy didn't know what to make of this. Did Eight plan to blow up the organization?

"I'm going to sleep," Eight declared. She stood up and tossed her dinner box over the railing and into the water.

Amy was outraged. "What did you do that for? You're polluting the ocean!"

Eight gave her a withering glance. "So call the garbage police," she said, picking up her pack and going to the stairs.

Well, Eight certainly had changed. And obviously she wasn't going to side with Amy against Five. Amy looked around. Five was huddled in conversation with Aly. Her Andy was talking to Andy Eleven, and Amy One was alone. Amy walked over to her and got right to the point.

"Are you worried about Amy Five?" she asked.

One looked alarmed. "Has she been flirting with my Andy?"

"No. I'm talking about the way she's acting like the boss of this trip."

One had something else on her mind. "Is he your boyfriend?" she asked Amy, looking at Andy Denker.

Amy wasn't sure what to call Andy. "He's a friend," she said carefully.

One nodded. "Just don't get him mixed up with *my* Andy, okay?"

"Not to worry," Amy murmured. She noticed that Five had left her position by Aly's side, and she went over. Aly scowled at her.

"I thought we were friends," the less perfect clone snapped.

"We are!" Amy said.

"Yeah, and that's why you tried to get me kicked off the boat!" With that, Aly picked up her box and moved to the other side of the deck.

At least now Andy was by himself. Amy One had dragged Andy Eleven away.

Amy went to sit by him. "Aly's such a baby," she fumed. "She really shouldn't be here."

Andy gave her that infuriating I'm-older-than-you-are look. "Actually, *you're* the one who's behaving childishly," he said. "You're jealous of Amy Five."

She was in no mood for a lecture. Angrily, she edged away from him, took out her Walkman, and clamped the headset over her ears. She got about ten seconds of moaning sounds, and then the contraption stopped. She jiggled the case, but that didn't help, and she let out a heartfelt groan.

"What's wrong?"

Amy Five actually seemed concerned. What a phony.

"My batteries are dead," Amy muttered.

"I know where you can get some fresh ones," Five said. "Come with me."

Uneasily, Amy followed Five to the helm, where the Devon android was at the wheel. "Excuse me," Five said politely to the android, and knelt down on the floor. Rolling up one leg of his trousers, she indicated a button above his ankle.

"They carry their own spares," she told Amy. When she pressed the button, a door in his leg flipped open, revealing a compartment that held rows of double-A batteries.

"You need one or two?" she asked Amy.

"Forget it." Amy wasn't about to accept favors from *her*.

Five closed the compartment. "Thank you," she told the android. To Amy she said, "If you change your mind, he's got enough for a month, and we won't be gone that long. They can change the batteries themselves, you know. They actually feel it when the batteries are starting to run down."

"How do *you* know so much about the androids?" Amy asked. She knew her voice was rude, but she couldn't help herself.

"Mr. Devon told me."

Amy's lips tightened. Mr. Devon had never told *her* anything about the androids. Without even thanking

Five, she marched away and plunked herself down on a deck chair away from everyone else. But she wasn't alone for long. Aly came over to her.

"I'm sorry I was so nasty before," she said. "We're all on the same side. And I think we should start talking about our plan for attacking the island."

Amy couldn't bring herself to look at her. The last thing she wanted was advice from a completely ordinary, unaltered clone. No, she realized, the last thing she wanted was to be on this trip.

f i 5 v e

So this was what it felt like to drown. Oddly enough, Amy wasn't in a panic. There was nothing she could do; there was no way she could save herself. Her wrists were bound so tightly, she knew she wouldn't be able to free them. Kicking might keep her afloat—but the blanket over her face was soaked through now, and even if she could keep her head above water, she'd suffocate under the weight of the blanket. And there was absolutely nothing in her genetically altered physical composition that would enable her to survive drowning and suffocation.

She would just have to let herself go. A drowsy sensation came over her, more powerful than the chill of the water. It was almost pleasant, like drifting off to sleep. Faces flickered through her mind—her mother, Tasha, Eric, Chris, Andy, Dr. Dave—blurring and blending into one warm feeling. . . .

Then there was another feeling. A strong arm, gripping her around the waist. A whoosh, a movement upward. Her face was free, and she gasped. She was dimly aware of cries and calls, words of praise and encouragement, and of being pulled up a rope ladder.

The next thing she knew, Andy was bent over her, pushing down on her chest, and pressing his lips against hers. A strange time to start kissing, she thought vaguely. Someone was twisting the rope around her wrists, and her hands were free. Then she was overcome by a fit of coughing. Andy moved back.

Amy struggled to sit up, and looked around. Her vision was still blurry from the water, but she made out the concerned faces that surrounded her. Two Andys, several Amys . . .

"What happened?" she managed to ask. But no one had to answer, because she knew. Someone had put a blanket over her head, bound her wrists, and thrown her into the ocean. Someone had tried to kill her. Someone—meaning one of *them*.

"Are you all right?" Andy asked her, and the anxiety in his face gave her a warm glow. "How do you feel?"

"Wet," Amy replied. "Very wet." She smiled. "Thank you for saving me."

Andy flushed. "It wasn't me," he admitted. "Amy Five saw you. She jumped in after you."

Amy turned her head slowly to look at Five. She, too, looked worried. But Amy wasn't stupid. "You pushed me in," she stated. "That's why you were the first to see me."

Five gasped. "Seven, no! Why would I do that?"

"Because you want to get rid of me!" Amy accused her. "Because you're afraid I'm going to take over!"

Five was a terrific actress, Amy thought. Actual tears sprang to her eyes.

"Amy, that's not true!" Andy cried. "If Five wanted to kill you, why would she jump in and save you?"

Amy had an answer for that. "To be a big hero. So everyone would admire her and think she's wonderful."

"No way," Aly said. "Five was with me when we both heard the splash."

Of course Aly would lie for Five, Amy thought. Five

was letting Aly stay on the boat. Then she realized her head was spinning and she was going to throw up.

She made it to the railing just in time. When she turned back around, the others were all huddled together, talking quietly. Plotting against her, maybe . . .

Five was pale but composed. "We're all upset and nervous and exhausted," she said. "I suggest we all go to sleep and talk about this in the morning."

Amy knew she herself wouldn't sleep a wink. For all she knew, Five was planning to come to her in the middle of the night and stick a pillow over her face. Even as she pulled the warm comforter over her shoulders a bit later and closed her eyes, she knew she wouldn't . . . sleep. . . .

When she opened her eyes again, sunlight streamed through the porthole. Amy One was talking to Amy Eight.

"Do you have a boyfriend?"

Eight's response was predictable. "None of your business."

"Okay . . . it's just that I thought I saw you looking at my Andy yesterday."

Eight rolled her eyes. "Oh, puh-leeze. I can do better than that." She turned away and left the room.

Aly was on the top bunk at the other side of the tiny room, and she turned to Amy. "How are you feeling?"

"Okay." Amy even offered Aly a half smile. After all, it couldn't possibly have been Aly who'd thrown her overboard. She didn't have that kind of strength. "Where's Five?"

"Probably up on deck."

Amy slipped out of bed and padded on bare feet up the stairs to the deck. Sure enough, Five was up there alone. She was leaning against a rail, staring out at the empty horizon. Amy joined her.

Five spoke first. "Look, I'm sorry if I've been pushing people around. I don't mean to act like the boss. But when I heard about stuff going on back at the island, I contacted Mr. Devon. He said I should try to get as many clones together as possible. So it was just sort of natural for me to take charge."

Amy didn't say anything at first. Five's voice was sincere, she sounded convincing, but . . .

"I just don't trust you," Amy said.

Five sighed. "Well, there's nothing I can do about that. But I promise you, I *swear* to you, I did *not* push you overboard. You have to believe me."

Amy had to admit that it could have been someone

else. Like One . . . Maybe she thought Amy had been making eyes at her boyfriend. Or Eight, who seemed to be in a perpetual bad mood. She didn't know much about Andy Eleven, either. . . . He could be a bad guy in disguise. Or the android . . .

She changed the subject. "Do you know when we'll reach the island?"

"Sometime today, I think. We should start figuring out a plan of action."

The others began appearing on deck, and the android brought them rolls and juice for breakfast. While they were eating, Andy Eleven got the first glimpse of land.

"There's the island," he announced. "I estimate it will take about four hours to reach it."

Everyone went to the railing and looked. Even with their supervision, they couldn't make out anything other than a patch of land in the distance.

Eight was the first to offer a proposal. "Let's attack."

Amy stared at her. "You mean just swim to shore and surprise them?"

"Sure, why not?"

"Because we need a plan," Amy said. "We have no idea how many people are there. And whether or not they have weapons. We can't just show up and expect them to surrender."

"Seven's right," Five said. "We need to know what's going on over there."

"Let's get closer," Andy Eleven suggested. "Then I can swim to shore and scout out the area."

"I'll go with you," Amy One said, but Eleven talked her out of that. It turned out Eleven was a champion swimmer, and he claimed he could swim really fast for over an hour. And no one should go with him. Alone on the island, he'd be able to move about quietly and keep hidden while he spied on the scene. Then he'd swim back to the boat and report the goings-on.

They all agreed that this was the best plan. So two hours later, Eleven donned a wet suit and prepared to dive in. "I'm figuring it will take me an hour to get there," he told them. "I'll spend an hour looking around and then head back. So I should return in about three hours."

"Be careful," Five said.

"I will." Eleven took her in his arms and planted a kiss on her lips. One shrieked.

Eleven jumped back. "Oops! Sorry, I thought you were my Amy." He turned, kissed One, and dived off the boat.

One was glaring at Five. "You did that on purpose!"

"Don't be silly," Amy reprimanded her. "It was a

mistake. Besides, it was *Eleven* who kissed *her*, not the other way around."

"You put yourself in a position to be kissed!" One accused Five. "You'd better stay away from my boyfriend, or I'll—I'll—" She didn't finish the threat, but it was clear that she was more than willing to fight for her Andy. Some girls could get absolutely crazy jealous when it came to their boyfriends. Now Amy was thinking that it really could have been One who had pushed her overboard, if One thought she was interested in Andy Eleven.

Her own Andy talked One down from her fury, and an uneasy calm came over the boat. There was nothing they could do until Eleven came back with his report.

"Thanks for defending me," Five said to Amy.

"You're welcome," Amy replied. "Thanks for saving my life."

"You're welcome," Five said.

Andy joined them. "I hope Eleven comes back when he said he will, or One's going to get hysterical."

"Isn't it amazing how we can all be so much alike yet so different?" Five mused.

Amy had to admit she'd often thought that herself. "Do you remember Annie Perrault, the French Amy?"

Five nodded. "Yeah, she gave me the creeps. I wonder if she's still on the island."

"Probably," Andy said. "She wouldn't even need the treatment to lose her emotions. That girl was evil." He turned to Amy. "Remember that sick group she was hanging with in the Paris Catacombs?"

It wasn't likely that Amy would ever forget that experience. Together she and Andy told Five about it. Five was impressed.

"You're lucky you escaped," she said. "Did you really push that Nazi guy off the Eiffel Tower?"

Amy nodded. "I can't remember his name."

Andy could. "Sebastien."

"Oh yeah. I guess we don't have to wonder what happened to him." She shuddered, thinking what he must have looked like when he hit the ground.

The group spent the afternoon playing cards, discussing favorite TV shows, and trying not to think about Eleven prowling around the island. One stayed down in the sleeping quarters, fretting and worrying and complaining about the others' not showing enough concern for Eleven. Of course, if any of the girls *had* shown any concern, One would have probably attacked her.

Five was the first to spot Eleven swimming back to

the boat. Her cry of joy brought them all to the rail. They watched as Eleven grabbed the rope ladder and climbed up to the deck. Andy gave him a hand and pulled him over the railing.

They gathered around him. "What did you see?" Aly asked.

"Nothing."

Disappointment settled heavily on the group. "You couldn't get close to them?" Amy asked.

"No, it wasn't that. I covered the whole island. No one's there. It's completely deserted."

That was unexpected news. Everyone was stunned. "But—but where are they?" Andy asked.

Eleven shrugged. "I guess they've packed up and moved on. They could be anywhere."

The clones stared at each other helplessly. Even Five was totally bewildered. "What do we do now?" she wondered.

"Give up," Eleven suggested. "Tell the android to turn this boat around, and let's go home."

"Sounds good to me," Eight said.

"No!" Aly cried out, and Amy too was shaking her head. But neither of them had any other suggestion to make. The deck was silent until Amy One appeared from downstairs.

"Andy!" she screamed, and flew into his arms. But this time, their kiss didn't last very long. One pulled back and pushed him away.

"What's the matter?" he asked her.

She wiped her mouth before replying. "You're not my Andy!"

six

Amy One's accusation rang in the air, and everyone was still. Five was the first to speak.

"How can you be sure?"

Amy One sniffed. "You think I don't know my own boyfriend's kiss?" She turned to wet-suit Andy in a fury. "Where is he? What have you done to my Andy?"

"I'm Andy Eleven," he insisted, but he was totally unconvincing. Amy One moved toward him threateningly, looking like she was ready to pounce, and he stepped back. "Hey, don't blame me. It wasn't my idea."

"Who are you?" Andy demanded to know.

"Number Six. They told me to swim here and pretend to be Eleven."

Amy tried to recall Andy Six, but nothing in particular came to mind. All she knew was that he'd been one of the first Andys to be voted off his survival team on their last visit to the island. So he'd had the treatment, and he was on the organization's side.

By now, Amy One was hysterical, shrieking at him. "Where is he? Did you hurt my Andy?"

"They won't hurt him," Andy Six said. "They want us alive and well. Doing what we're supposed to do."

Five looked at him, hard. "*They!* You're talking about the organization, right?"

He nodded. "If that's what you call them. The guys in charge. And the chick, what's her name—Cindy."

For someone who was supposedly on the other side, he seemed all too willing to provide information. But it occurred to Amy that this made sense. With no emotions, there could be no loyalties. The treated clones would respond to whoever appeared to be in charge. Here, on this boat, *they* were the people in charge.

"So the organization told you to tell us not to come to the island," she said. "How come? Don't they want us?"

"Not particularly," Andy Six replied. "I mean, if you

want to come and be a part of us, fine. But if you're going to interfere, they want you to stay away."

Five looked at Amy. "Which means they're satisfied with the clones they have now, and don't need us."

Amy nodded. "Which also means they're using the acceleration process. Is that right?" she asked Andy Six.

He looked blank, and she realized he probably didn't know about the procedure. Just like no one knew about the emotion treatment until it was given.

Now Amy One was sobbing. "They're going to take Andy's emotions away. He's not going to love me anymore."

No one even tried to reassure her. They all knew it was probably true.

"How many clones are on the island?" Andy asked him.

"There're four Andys—five, counting Eleven."

"No, there're still only four," Aly pointed out. "You're here."

"Oh yeah, that's right."

"How many Amys?" Five asked.

"I don't know. They keep the boys and the girls separate."

"That doesn't make sense," Aly said. "I mean, I thought they wanted the boys and girls to get together."

"They're waiting for us to grow up more," Amy told her. "But if they've got this acceleration thing happening, that's only going to take a day or two."

"Which means we've got to stop them now," Five said. "Let's figure this out. He says there are four Andys, and we know that four Amys were left behind. So that means there are at least eight clones. Plus organization people."

"We're stronger than they are," Andy said. "But what about the Devon clones? I remember they were pretty strong."

"There aren't many of them around anymore," Andy Six volunteered.

"Where'd they go?" Five asked.

"I don't know. Maybe they left. Maybe they're dead."

He didn't seem to care one way or the other. But that made sense too. Why would he care about Devon clones when he had no feelings? Amy imagined a world of people without feelings, and she shivered.

"We're six," she said. "Not counting *him*."

Five knew who she meant. "We could use him, though. He's got the physical powers."

"But he could use them for the other side," Amy pointed out. "We can't count on him."

She didn't have any problem talking about Andy Six

right in front of his face. He wasn't paying any attention to the conversation anyway. He was staring at Aly.

"I want your earrings," he said suddenly, and reached toward her ears. Aly stepped back in alarm. But this gave Amy an idea.

"You need pierced ears to wear them," she told Andy Six. "Anyone got a needle?"

"What are you doing?" Five asked her in a whisper.

"If we don't know which side he'll choose, it's better if he has no powers at all," Amy whispered back.

It turned out that One had a little sewing kit with her. And Andy Six was perfectly willing to let someone pierce his earlobes so he could wear Aly's little hoops.

They kept their eyes on him, because it would take a while for his powers to disappear. But by the time they reached the island, he would be completely ordinary.

seven 7

Under the cover of darkness, around one in the morning, the lifeboat hit the shore. The seven occupants climbed out. Carrying her shoes, Amy could feel the warm, soft sand under her bare feet, and it brought back a clear memory of her last time on this island. It was familiar and frightening at the same time. She wondered if the others were feeling as strange as she was. They too had been here before.

Andy Six stumbled and bumped into her. "I can't see where I'm going," he grumbled. Amy smiled. His vision wasn't what it used to be, and this meant all his genetic superiority was dissipating rapidly. He wouldn't be any use to them, but at least he wouldn't be any use to the organization, either.

She could see that memories of the island were still fresh for everyone, even Aly, although she too needed some help finding her way in the dark. The others moved with the same confidence Amy did, each recognizing the large rocks that formed a set of stairs. At the top of the stairway, they could see a path made of tiny pebbles, leading toward some leafy trees. Then came more trees, closer together, and soon after, they were in the woods. Amy knew that when they emerged from the woods, they would encounter a wall of rocks. What she couldn't be sure of was what they'd see this time on the other side of the wall.

They'd heard nothing usual so far, so she assumed that everyone on the island was asleep. Peering through a crack in the wall confirmed this—the enclosure was dark, with no sign of life.

Andy Six had said the males and females were separated, just as they'd been the last time. That hadn't prevented them from finding ways to come together, though. Amy remembered meeting *her* Andy in a grotto, a small cave cut into the stone behind a thick patch of wavy rushes.

He remembered too—she knew from the way he suddenly turned to her and smiled.

"We should split up," Aly whispered.

"Why?" Eight asked. "I think we should stay together. Safety in numbers, united we stand, and all that."

Five agreed with Aly. "We'll make too much noise moving around in a group. Besides, there's too much ground to cover." She took a branch that had fallen from a tree and drew an outline of the island. Amy found another branch, and together they made marks indicating the places they remembered from their stay. The girls' cabins, the boys' cabins, the labyrinth, the organization building with its underground floors.

"What's that?" Eight asked when Amy drew a snaky line coming out from the building.

"The tunnel from the organization building that leads to the beach," Amy said.

"It wasn't there," Eight told her. "It was on the other side."

Amy frowned. "Are you sure? That doesn't seem right."

"I'm absolutely positively sure," Eight declared.

Not wanting to start an argument, Amy wiped out the line she'd drawn and placed another where Eight was pointing. But she kept in mind the original line.

Maybe all the clones weren't equal in their ability to remember things precisely.

Then they formed teams to scout different areas. Amy was teamed with Five and Eight; Andy would take Aly and One and drag Andy Six along with him. They designated areas of the island for each team to explore and established a meeting place where they could share information at a set time a few hours away. Then they took off in opposite directions.

For a while, Amy walked silently between Five and Eight along the side of the wall until they reached the opening. There, however, they had to enter single file, and a decision had to be made: who would lead? Amy and Five looked at each other with challenge in their eyes. But Eight ignored them and strode on through the opening into the enclosure, leaving Amy wondering if Five felt as silly as she did.

The area seemed silent and deserted. In accordance with the plan, they started in the direction of the organization building. They all knew the way, and walked together until they reached the wooded area that surrounded the building. Again, the path was too narrow for three to walk side by side.

But there were no awkward pauses this time. Amy

caught a glimpse of something moving out of the corner of her eye.

Five noticed it too. "Was it an animal?" she asked Amy in a whisper.

"I don't think so," Amy said. She turned to Eight. "What did it look like to you?"

Eight looked uncertain. "I don't know. No one's supposed to be here. . . . I mean, I wasn't expecting to see anyone out here. Now. So late at night."

She was rambling in a confused way, and Amy looked at her curiously. But then Five grabbed her arm. "It's a person. A woman."

"Cindy?" Amy wondered aloud.

Whoever it was had become aware of their presence. Amy could see the figure now, crouching behind a thick shrub, obviously trying to hide.

Amy kept her voice low. "We can corner her there."

Eight agreed. "Yeah. Then we jump her and I'll hit her on the head with my backpack."

"But that could kill her!" Five exclaimed softly.

"So what?" Eight asked.

Amy was aghast. What had happened to this girl to make her so violent? And she was so casual about it! Exchanging glances with Five, Amy knew Five was thinking the same thing. And for once, Amy was glad to have a companion as strong as *she* was, to keep Eight from acting on her impulses.

They moved closer to the figure. In unspoken agreement, Amy and Five separated so they could approach her from different sides. At the same time, they both kept an eye on Eight.

The woman saw Five first. She leaped up and turned to run in the opposite direction—and found herself face to face with Amy. She gasped. And so did Amy. This wasn't Cindy, but she looked very, very familiar.

The woman must have realized she had no chance to escape from the three Amys, so she just stood there, her bright brown eyes darting from one face to another. She didn't appear to be shocked to find three identical girls confronting her. But she did seem awed by the sight.

Amy was in awe too. She'd figured out why the woman looked so familiar. She'd seen her face before—in a mirror, on her own thirteenth birthday. This woman was an adult version of herself—of all of them.

As she moved closer, Amy saw that the woman was

older than Amy had been when she'd aged. This woman looked to be around the age of Nancy Candler. Then Amy knew who the woman had to be, and her heart sank.

"She's an accelerated clone," she told Five and Eight. "They've started the process."

eight

After only an hour of exploring, Andy was fed up. If he hadn't known how important it was to remain silent, he would have screamed at the top of his lungs, just to release his tension. Why, *why* had he ever agreed to this division of teams?

Actually, he knew why. He was sick and tired of the power struggle between Amy Seven and Amy Five. And even though they seemed to have come to terms with a kind of joint leadership, he was still annoyed with them. These Amys always wanted to be in charge. It never occurred to them that *he* might want to be the leader.

With this smaller group, he was definitely in command, but it wasn't much of an army. Amy One wouldn't stop whining. All she talked about was finding Andy Eleven, as if no one else on the island mattered. Andy Six was worthless. Having him around was like dragging a suitcase full of stuff you didn't really need. As his powers diminished, he lagged behind, and Andy and Amy One were always having to push him to keep going. It was only basic human integrity that kept Andy from dumping him somewhere and letting him fend for himself.

Aly was trying to be cooperative. At least she had a good attitude. But she couldn't keep up with them, not even with Andy Six, and she was already getting very tired. She put on a brave face and kept moving, but Andy could see the fatigue in her eyes.

They were nearing cabins now. "How many of these are occupied?" Andy asked Six.

"I don't know. These are the girls' cabins."

The organization didn't have all the Amys, so some of the cabins had to be empty, Andy thought—unless acceleration had already begun, as well as the mating between the male and female clones. For all he knew, these cabins were now filled with the next generation of Amys and Andys.

"Stay here," he instructed the others. Alone, he moved silently toward the cabins. If he could locate an empty one, they could take a break inside, and Aly could sleep.

He approached the closest cabin first, number eight. Peering through the window, he could see a bed—with an occupant. At least, he assumed that the lump wrapped in a blanket was a person. He couldn't see the face, but the hair was brown, like most of the Amys'.

He moved on to the next cabin. This one was occupied too—but here he had a clear look at the person inside. She was sitting on her bed, looking out the window on the opposite side of the room. This gave Andy a three-quarter profile of her face, and he gasped.

For a second, he thought he was looking at his mother, Eve Carrington. Then she moved slightly, her face becoming clear in the moonlight, and he knew it wasn't her. This woman was younger . . . in her twenties, he estimated. But he could see why he had mistaken her for his mother. This woman too was an adult version of Amy.

So the acceleration process had begun. This woman was definitely old enough to bear children. Now he had something to report to the others.

He retreated silently, before she could turn and see

him. He didn't know that Andy Six had followed him until he stepped on the boy's foot.

"Ow!" Six yelled.

"Shut up," Andy whispered, but it was too late. The noise had alerted the woman, who moved to the window. She was looking straight at them.

Andy froze. What would she do—scream? Send out an alarm?

She must have been in shock, because at first she did nothing. She just stood at the window, gazing steadily at the two boys standing outside.

She was beautiful.

Andy went to the door and turned the handle. It wasn't locked. When he went into the room, she stepped back, obviously apprehensive.

"Hello," Andy said.

She said nothing. He went closer. "You—you're one of the Amys, aren't you?"

She bowed her head slightly, as if in affirmation.

"Which one?" he asked.

She didn't answer. He went even closer, and now he could see her eyes. There was something in them . . . fear?

"I won't hurt you," he said.

Her eyes shifted to the second boy, now standing in the doorway. Andy turned to him. "Go back to the others," he ordered him.

Andy Six obeyed.

Turning back to the woman, Andy asked, "Did they accelerate you? Is that what happened?"

Still, he got no response. And the fear hadn't left her eyes. It dawned on him that he had no idea about the side effects of the acceleration process. Maybe the clones lost their powers—and maybe even some of the abilities they would have had as ordinary people.

"Can you speak?" he asked.

She didn't nod or shake her head. He knew she wasn't deaf, because she had heard them outside, but she could be mute.

Her eyes were speaking for her. There was less fear in them now, as if she'd assessed Andy and decided he wouldn't hurt her. A new expression filled her eyes. She seemed to be asking for something. No, it was more than asking. She was pleading.

Had she been captured and brought here by force? The more he looked at her, the more he felt sure that this was the case. She seemed so helpless and lost. The fear he'd seen earlier must have been because she thought he was one of the island Andys. Now she was realizing that he didn't present any danger to her. That he could save her.

"It's okay," he said. "I can help you. Come with me." He held out his hand, and she placed her own delicate hand in his.

She seemed to take some reassurance from his touch. And she left the cabin with him.

nine

"Do you know who she is?" Five asked Amy in an undertone. The older woman was now seated with them on some rocks that surrounded what looked like the remains of a campfire. Eight produced a lighter, and they managed to get a small fire going again. There was a chill in the night air, and they all drew close together.

Amy knew what Five meant. The woman was obviously an accelerated Amy, but which one? She shook her head. "I don't even think *she* knows."

At first, when they'd found her, the woman had seemed stunned and confused. She couldn't tell them her name, or what she was doing on the island. Now, almost two hours later, she just seemed a little dazed, as if she was recovering from some traumatic experience. Having been accelerated herself, Amy could relate.

She moved to sit down next to the woman. "I know, it's weird," she said sympathetically. "You wake up one day, you look in the mirror, and you see a stranger."

The woman gazed at her with a puzzled expression. "I don't understand you."

"Did it hurt?" Eight asked. "Getting accelerated, I mean. Did they stick you with lots of needles?"

The woman's face didn't clear. "I don't know. I guess I just don't understand. . . ."

"You don't understand what?" Five asked.

The woman gestured vaguely. "I don't understand what's going on."

"Do you think you might have lost your memory?" Amy asked her.

The woman actually brightened. "Yes! That would explain everything, wouldn't it?"

"We need more wood for this fire," Five said sud-

70

denly. She was looking directly at the woman. "Could you toss me that big log next to you?"

The woman glanced to her side and saw the log Five was talking about. She reached over to pick it up, but she could barely budge it. It was way too heavy for her to lift. Then Amy knew why Five had asked her to get it. It was a test. And unless the woman was faking the effort, she did not have the strength the genetically altered clones had.

Amy didn't think it was an act. The woman had such a nice face, and Amy wasn't thinking this just because the face was so much like her own. There was an air about her that made Amy feel something. She didn't know how to describe the sensation. She was . . . she felt . . . comfortable. Which was not how she usually felt with a complete stranger.

So if the woman had no unusual powers . . . She exchanged a look with Five, who nodded. Eight said out loud what all three of them were thinking: "Does this mean you lose your powers when you get accelerated?"

"Maybe," Five told her. "Hey, don't look so depressed! This is good news. If the organization knows this will happen, they won't want to accelerate the rest of the clones. It would ruin any plan for a master race."

"But I didn't lose my powers when I aged," Amy told her.

"Maybe it doesn't happen right away," Five said. She turned to the woman. "How long have you been like this?"

The woman looked at her with a helpless smile.

"Oh, right," Five said. "You have no memory. Well, there's probably an answer somewhere, but I'm too wiped out to think about it now."

"I'm tired too," Amy agreed. "I guess we'll just have to camp out here. I wish we had sleeping bags." She looked at the ground in distaste. "Maybe we can gather some leaves for a bed."

"That won't be necessary," the woman said suddenly. "I remember something. A place where I've been sleeping." She got up and beckoned the girls to follow.

"I don't like this," Eight said uneasily. "We don't know anything about this woman. She could be leading us into a trap."

It was a possibility. But somehow, Amy didn't believe that was the case. And Five was going along with it too. Besides, what did they have to fear from a woman with no powers? The three of them could easily restrain her if necessary.

There was no need, though. Amy recognized where the woman was taking them. "Those are the cabins we stayed in!" Amy said.

The woman showed them the one where she was staying, and Five peeked through the window of the one next to it. "It's empty," she reported.

Five and Eight went inside, but Amy accompanied the woman into her cabin. She looked around.

"Is there anything here that might bring back your memory?" she asked.

"I don't think so," the woman said. "Feel free to look around if you like."

Amy looked in the closet, where she saw a few items of clothing, not much else. The dresser drawer held a nightgown and some lingerie. On the top of the dresser was a silver watch. It looked like an expensive one, and on an impulse, Amy picked it up and looked at the back of the face. In tiny letters, there was an inscription.

She read it out loud. "For Eve, from Mom and Dad."

The woman put a hand to her mouth, as if to stifle a gasp.

"Is that your name?" Amy asked her. "Eve? Shouldn't it be Amy?"

"I'm not sure," the woman said carefully. "Amy sounds

right, I guess. I must have found that watch on the beach."

"Eve," Amy repeated. "It's a pretty name. Well, good night. I guess I'll see you in the morning." She put the watch back on the dresser and left to go to the cabin next door.

ten 10

It was still dark when Amy woke up, and she had the feeling she hadn't been sleeping very long. Eight was sitting at the edge of her bed, and Amy realized she'd been shaken awake.

"I saw something," Eight said.

Amy rubbed her eyes. "Where?"

"Outside. I couldn't sleep, so I took a walk. I saw someone going into a cave. We should follow him."

Her shrill, nervous voice had woken Five, too. She sat up in bed. "What did he look like?"

"Kind of tall, and dark. He wasn't one of our group, I know that. Come on, let's go."

Amy yawned. "Can't we follow him in the morning?"

But Eight was insistent. "That could be too late! Right now, they don't know we're here. We could take them by surprise."

Five got out of bed. "I guess it wouldn't hurt to do some investigating."

There was no way Amy would let Five appear to be more aggressive than *she* was. All desire to sleep vanished and she too got out of bed.

"I'm ready."

Outside, she and Five let Eight take the lead for once, and they followed her in the direction she'd taken her walk. She led them back into the forest, walking determinedly toward a hilly area. She seemed to have no trouble remembering exactly where the cave was.

"He went in there," she said, pointing. Amy hesitated. Who knew what could be waiting for them inside? But Eight marched right on in, and Five followed, so Amy had no choice but to march into the cave too.

It seemed empty at first. Eight spotted a low archway that opened into a tunnel. "He went this way," she declared, and got down on her hands and knees to crawl through.

Amy wondered how Eight could have possibly known this, since she'd only seen him go into the cave and she couldn't have seen the tunnel from the outside. But she got down on her hands and knees, along with Five, and the three crawled inside.

They didn't have to crawl very long. The tunnel widened into a concrete corridor. Amy felt her skin crawl. She was reminded of the hallways under the organization building, mazes that had trapped them. She was getting increasingly uneasy, but she didn't want Five to know, so she kept moving. They reached a door.

Five tried the handle. "It's locked."

"Knock," Eight said impatiently.

"Are you crazy?" Five asked. "We don't want to tell them we're coming!"

Eight shoved her aside and rapped hard on the door. It was immediately opened by a tall, dark-haired man. . . .

"Mr. Devon?" But even as she said the name, Amy could see that this wasn't the real Mr. Devon. He wasn't a Devon android, either, because he was talking.

He wasn't saying anything coherent, though. What came out of his mouth was gibberish, noises with an occasional recognizable word. He was disheveled, and his clothes were in rags. He didn't react at all to finding them at the door. He just turned and shuffled away.

"He must be one of the Devon clones," Five said. "What happened to him?"

"They were experiments," Eight told her. "Cloned from Mr. Devon and then accelerated. They were fine for a while, then they went crazy and died. That's probably the last one, and he's about to drop."

"How do you know this?" Amy asked.

"Mr. Devon told me."

Five frowned. "He never told *me* about this."

"Me either," Amy said. She thought about Eve, the accelerated clone. Would she end up like this too? Or had the organization worked out these acceleration problems by now?

Another figure appeared at the end of the hall. It was an Amy. She didn't seem alarmed when she saw them, but that was probably more emotion than she could manage.

"What do you want?" she asked.

Amy and Five opened their mouths at the same time to respond, but Eight beat them to it. "Take us to your leader," she said.

Amy thought she sounded like a character in an old, bad science-fiction movie, but the Amy at the end of the hall only nodded. "Come with me."

She waited for them, and then turned down another corridor. Which one is she? Amy wondered as they followed her. She tried to remember the numbers of the clones who had stayed behind on the island.

Five was apparently having the same thoughts. "What's your number?" she asked.

"Eight," the clone replied.

"Eight?" Five repeated. "You can't be Eight. *She's* Eight."

A cold sensation began to travel up Amy's spine. "What's your name?"

"Amy Sherman."

"From Brooklyn, New York?"

"Yes."

Five turned to the Amy who had led them in there. "Then who are you?"

A look of smug satisfaction spread across the face of the Amy they'd been calling Number Eight. "*I* am Number Ten," she replied. "Aimee Evans."

"The actress?" Amy asked in disbelief.

She nodded. "Obviously. You can see how well I impersonated Number Eight."

Amy grabbed Five's arm. "It's a trap. We have to get out of here."

But it was too late. A door opened. Eight and Ten pushed them through it and followed them in. The door slammed shut with an ominous bang.

In the room, a figure stepped out of the shadows.

"This is our leader," Eight announced.

It took every bit of Amy's self-control to keep herself from screaming. Because the last time she'd seen this man, he had been plummeting from the top of the Eiffel Tower.

eleven

"Andy, where are we going?" Aly asked. She was getting cranky. The lack of sleep was taking its toll on all of them.

"And why are we going with *her*?" Amy One demanded.

For the hundredth time, Andy tried to explain. It wasn't an easy question to answer, because he wasn't sure himself why he was so willing to follow the silent adult Amy to wherever she was leading them. "Because—because she knows something. She's a clue."

"But she's one of *them*," Aly reminded him. "She could be taking us to the organization."

"Well, we have to confront them sooner or later," Andy said. "At least she'll get us into the building. Besides, I don't think she's on their side. She didn't do anything while we were sleeping. I think she's trying to escape from them."

Aly rolled her eyes. "How do you know that? She certainly couldn't have told you. The woman can't speak."

"I can *feel* it," Andy said helplessly. The adult Amy turned and gave him a brilliant smile. To Aly he added, "We shouldn't talk about her like this. She may not speak, but she can hear us."

"You're no help!" Aly shouted at the woman. The woman didn't look fazed. "She's dead weight, Andy."

Andy didn't care. The fact that the woman couldn't speak only added to the mystery that made her so appealing.

Amy One gave him a reproving look. "She's too old for you, Andy."

"For crying out loud, I'm not in love with her," Andy said, but in his heart he wondered if he was telling the truth. She was so lovely. And helpless. She couldn't escape on her own. She needed him to fight the organization for her.

Andy Six joined the conversation. "Besides, she won't be too old for him much longer. When they accelerate him, he'll be the same age she is."

"What does an adult Andy look like?" Amy One asked him.

"I don't know. They haven't accelerated any of us yet."

Andy had been wondering the same thing. What would he look like ten or fifteen years older? A lot of physical changes took place in that much time. He hoped this Amy would like the way he looked. Then he realized what he was thinking, and was horrified.

What was the matter with him? He wasn't going to be accelerated, and neither were the rest of them. They'd fight the organization, and they would win. He'd take this accelerated Amy to Dr. Hopkins back in Los Angeles, and soon she'd be back to normal. Only she wouldn't be like Amy Seven and Five, who were totally independent. She'd stay sweet and helpless. And he'd learn sign language so they could communicate. And then they'd—

Aly interrupted his daydream. "What is she doing?"

They had reached a hilly area, and the adult Amy had gotten down on her hands and knees. She seemed to be looking for something. Suddenly, she rose, and with a clear expression of panic on her face, she pointed.

Andy bent down to look. "There's a cave here."

"And she's scared to death of whatever is in it," One said. "Let's get out of here."

"No," Andy said firmly. "If this leads us to the organization, then this is where we need to go." To the accelerated Amy he said, "Don't worry, I'll be with you. I'll protect you." He knew not to expect a response, but something about his manner seemed to give her strength. She managed a brave little smile.

"Well, I'm not going anywhere till I get some more sleep," Aly declared. "I'm not going to try to fight the organization when I'm completely wiped out."

"Me too," Amy One declared. She plunked herself down on a patch of moss. "I'm taking a nap right here."

Aly joined her. "Me too."

"I could use some sleep," Andy Six said.

Andy frowned. He was the leader of this group. He couldn't leave them here while he and the adult Amy explored the cave.

"Okay, we'll take a one-hour break," he said. He gestured to the adult Amy and pointed to the others lying on the ground. For a moment, he thought he saw a flash of annoyance in her eyes, but then she nodded obediently and sat down on the moss.

It was the right decision. Along with the others, she fell asleep.

Andy was tired too, but he couldn't sleep. This woman . . . stirred him in a way he'd never experienced before. She made him feel strong and powerful. And she was so beautiful. He knew that this was how Amy Seven would look when she was older, and that this was how his mother must have looked when she was young. Somehow, in some mysterious way, it all came together to present the most appealing woman he'd ever seen. He couldn't take his eyes off her face.

Her lips moved, and a soft, barely audible sound came from them. He watched in amazement. She was talking in her sleep! Was it possible that she could speak? Maybe it was the psychological trauma of acceleration that made her deaf and mute! He crept closer to hear what she was saying.

But the words didn't make any sense at first. They were only sounds. He leaned over her, practically pressing his ear against her mouth. His brow furrowed. No, they weren't just sounds. They were words. But not in English.

The adult Amy was speaking French.

A horrible realization swept over him, followed by a wave of nausea. At that moment, he knew who she was.

"Annie," he whispered. "Annie Perrault." The ballerina. The evil clone he'd met in Paris. The one who had belonged to the neo-Nazi group in the Catacombs, the group who wanted to destroy everyone they considered imperfect.

"Annie," he whispered again.

Her eyes opened. And suddenly, she was on top of him, pinning him to the ground. He struggled to free himself, but age had made her stronger than he was. He yelled, and the others woke up.

Andy Six just sat there and watched with interest, but Aly and Amy One tried to pull her off him. They weren't any help, though, since Aly had no strength and One wasn't as strong as Annie.

Even in his horror and fear, Andy felt disappointment. He'd been so completely wrong about her. What kind of an idiot was he, anyway?

He continued to try to break her grip on him, but the situation seemed hopeless. Then he heard Amy One cry out.

"Mr. Devon!"

The hope returned. He'd help them, he'd do something. He wasn't a clone with superstrength, but maybe he had a gun or some other weapon.

Andy caught a glimpse of the man. He *did* have a gun! "You're history," he told Annie Perrault.

But once again, appearances were deceiving. Annie released him—but Andy realized that the gun wasn't pointed at her.

"On your feet," Devon barked. He was talking to Andy.

Bewilderment was followed by total disillusionment. For all his years, Andy had thought Devon was a bad guy. Only recently had he come to believe that Devon really was on his side.

But he'd been tricked again. And as he rose and joined Aly and Amy One with his hands raised, he didn't feel only fear. He felt like a fool.

twelve 12

"I hate guns," Amy muttered. That was what they were facing—a gun, a weapon even genetically superior clones couldn't protect themselves from. Bullets moved too fast for even them to stop. She and Five could only sit on the concrete floor and do what they were ordered to do.

The guns were held by Amys and Andys. Their very own brothers and sisters! Of course, those clones couldn't feel the emotions of a fraternal bond. They couldn't feel at all.

The door opened. The organization leader, the bizarre Sebastien, who had survived the Eiffel Tower fall, was the first to enter. He was followed by Andys Five and Six, Aly, and Amy One. Behind them was an adult Amy, but younger than the one Amy had met. She said something to Sebastien in French, and with a feeling of revulsion, Amy knew right away who she was.

Her own adult Amy—Eve—wasn't there, and Amy could only hope that she had escaped, or at least was still successfully hiding. Behind them, with another gun, was someone who looked like Mr. Devon. One of the androids, she assumed.

Amy One took a look at the crew who were holding them hostage and burst out crying. "Andy! Andy, it's me! Why are you doing this?"

Four boys looked at her impassively. She was only talking to one—the Andy she'd recognized as Number Eleven. It was uncanny, the way she could pick out her boyfriend from among these identical guys. But he didn't respond any differently than the others. He'd obviously had the emotion treatment, which meant he didn't— couldn't—love her anymore.

Sebastien was rubbing his hands together, looking extremely pleased with himself. He spoke to them in English, with a thick accent.

"Hello, my friends," he said. "Do not be afraid. Zees eez where you belong." To Aimee he said, "I believe you haff somesing for me."

Aimee took off her backpack and handed it to him.

"What's in there?" Five asked Amy in a whisper.

"Weapons and bombs," Amy said in a resigned voice. She'd known that all along, but she'd thought the weapons were for them to use.

She couldn't believe she'd actually bought into Aimee's impersonation of Amy Eight. Aimee was a terrible actress, and there had been so many times when Amy had thought Eight was behaving unlike herself. Why hadn't she picked up on the fraud? Well, at least Five hadn't figured it out either.

Carrying the backpack, Sebastien left the room, followed by the android Devon. Amy's own Andy slumped on the floor beside her. He had recognized Sebastien too.

"I don't get it," he said. "He fell off the Eiffel Tower! No one could survive that, not even one of us."

"He is better than us," Annie Perrault informed him. Now that she had a voice, she wasn't so pretty anymore, Andy thought.

"What do you mean, 'better'?" Amy asked. "What is he? An android? A clone?"

Annie smiled—and that wasn't pretty anymore either. "He is something very, very special. Unique. One of a kind. His brain is human, but the genes that determine his mental abilities have been altered far beyond ours. His body is artificial, controlled by the brain through advanced electronic impulses. He does not need to eat, or sleep, or do anything that humans need to do. And nothing can hurt him. He is invulnerable."

"And he's the actual head of the organization?" Aly asked.

"Yes." There was unmistakable pride in her tone. "We French have surpassed you Americans. As we often do. Even without technologies, my people are naturally superior."

"Is that true?" Aly asked Amy. "You've been to France."

"Only in cooking," Amy assured her. She was thinking about numbers now. The organization had five Andys, three ordinary Amys, and an accelerated Amy. Plus, they had Sebastien—and who knew what other organization members might be lurking around? Her side had three regular Amy clones, and maybe one accelerated Amy, if Eve showed up. They had one clone with no power, and one regular Andy. It didn't look promising for the good guys.

She turned to Andy. "I wonder how many Devon androids they have?"

"That wasn't a Devon android," Andy told her. "He talked. It was either a clone or the real Mr. Devon."

"He couldn't have been a clone," Amy said. "They're all either dead or crazy." But she refused to believe that the gun-toting Devon look-alike was the real man. Maybe he was just pretending to be on their side, and he had a plan.

Five spoke to Aimee. "If Sebastien is so perfect and invulnerable, how come you had to bring him bombs and stuff?"

"I wasn't carrying bombs," Aimee said. "I just told Seven that."

"Why?" Amy asked.

"Because I wanted to scare you. You were asking too many questions and you're too smart. I thought you might take over and figure everything out."

Amy couldn't help feeling just a little satisfaction in knowing that Five heard that. "So you're the one who tried to drown me?" she said accusingly.

"That's right. I thought it was best to get you out of the way. Too bad Five felt the need to save you."

"Well, I am alive," Amy spat out. "And soon you'll be

the one who gets taken down. What's in your precious bag?"

"Shut up," Annie Perrault barked. But she was looking at Aimee when she said that, not at Amy.

Aimee glared at her. "Don't tell me to shut up. Who do you think you are?"

"I am older than you are," Annie said. "And I am French."

"Big deal," Aimee said. "*I'm* a movie star." To Amy, she said, "Batteries."

"Batteries?" Aly asked.

"Yeah, Sebastien needs them."

So he had something in common with a regular android, Amy thought. That meant he wasn't completely invulnerable. But the backpack must contain hundreds of batteries. He had enough juice to keep himself operating for a long, long time.

One of the treated Andys spoke to Andy Six. "Where did you get those earrings?"

"From her," Six said, indicating Aly.

Aly perked up. "Would you like to have pierced ears too?" she asked hopefully.

"Yeah," the boy said, but Annie Perrault shook her head.

"Your earlobes must never be pierced. You will lose your powers."

"So *that's* what happened to me," Andy Six said. "Can I be fixed?"

"Of course," Annie said. "Take the earrings out. Eventually, the hole will close."

"But they look so cool," Andy Six grumbled. Still, he did as he was told. Amy gave Aly an encouraging smile. It had been a good idea to disable the entire group with a session of ear piercing. But it wasn't going to work.

For a moment, Aly looked deflated. Then a new expression spread over her face.

She spoke to Annie. "So, I guess you guys have won, huh? You're really going to create a master race."

"Yes, we are," Annie said.

"You want some help?"

"Aly!" Amy and Five exclaimed simultaneously.

"Sorry, guys," Aly said. "But I can see now that you're all losers. I want to be on the side of the winners."

Annie smiled. She turned to one of the armed clones. "Amy Four, would you take her to Sebastien?"

Four came over and took Aly's arm. Together they started out.

Amy was bewildered. What was Aly doing? Surely

she wasn't really planning to go over to the other side. They wouldn't want her anyway; she didn't have the right genes.

Then Amy noticed something tossed casually around Aly's shoulder. A Walkman.

Amy looked at her own bag, lying on the floor next to her, and realized that it was open. And her Walkman was missing.

Apparently, even without superior genes, Aly could come up with some bright ideas.

thirteen 13

At least the organization wasn't planning to starve them. Boxed lunches were brought in by a pink-smocked girl. So they're still around, Amy thought. These girls were the results of an early effort at cloning, which had resulted in a bunch of placid, zombielike creatures.

Opening the box, she saw the same meal she'd had yesterday on the boat: a chicken sandwich, pasta salad, chips, an apple, and a chocolate bar. Andy Six sauntered over to Amy.

"I want your chocolate bar," he said. "Give it to me."

"No way," Amy retorted.

"But I want it."

"Too bad, you can't have it."

Six tried to stick his hand in the box. Amy grabbed his wrist and pulled him to the ground. He didn't have his powers back yet, so she was able to pin him down. Not that it did her much good. One order from Annie and a gun-toting Andy pulled Amy off him.

But at least she'd had some effect on him, even if it was only a minor injury. His arm had come into contact with Lulu's necklace, and one of the sharper horse teeth had jabbed him. It wasn't much of a cut—only a few drops of blood oozed out—but Andy Six whimpered and carried on like he'd been mortally wounded. He crept off to a corner of the room and curled up like a baby, nursing his arm.

"You are such a pain," Annie said to Amy. "I should have you shot right now."

"You'd have to go through me," Andy said, positioning himself in front of Amy. "Do you really want to lose *two* healthy genetically superior clones?"

Annie scowled at him, but said no more. She left the room, probably to go eat a superior French meal with Sebastien. No, Sebastien didn't eat. Maybe he'd just have a glass of wine.

Meanwhile, Amy was more interested in what Andy had said.

"Andy! Would you really be willing to die for me?"

"If you'd let me," Andy replied.

"What's *that* supposed to mean?"

"Do you really have to be so stubborn and independent *all* the time?" he asked. "Can't you lean on me once in a while? Not that I want to be macho, but I wouldn't mind feeling like a man once in a while."

Amy had to smile. "Look, if we get out of this and survive, I promise I'll lean on you for five minutes every day. How's that?"

He grinned. "Well, it's better than nothing. And it's not like I want you to turn into an Amy One."

Amy One was now attempting to revive Andy Eleven's emotions. She was gazing up at the stoic boy with a flirty expression on her face.

"Andy . . . remember when we were here on the island before, and we used to meet late at night down by the beach?"

"Yes, I remember," he said.

"And remember when my parents were sleeping and you sneaked into my room?"

"I remember that, too," he said. "So what?"

"Doesn't that *mean* anything to you?" she practically wailed.

"No."

Amy went over and put her arm around One. "Give up," she said, as kindly as she could. "There's nothing you can do. It's a DNA thing. This emotion treatment revives a dormant gene that made the earliest form of man oblivious to everything but his own survival. Eleven's not capable of caring about you."

"But why are they doing this to us?" One wept.

"So we'll follow orders, and not listen to what our heart tells us, or our conscience."

One raised a tear-stained face. "I don't want to be like that," she said.

"None of us do," Amy told her. She glanced at the treated clones. "Not even them."

One of *them*—Amy Four—returned with Aly. She pushed Aly back to her position on the floor. Amy crouched down next to her.

"Are you okay?"

Aly nodded, but she winced when Amy put her hand on her shoulder. "Sebastien got mad when he found out I wasn't so perfect."

Amy wanted to cry and kick herself. She'd actually

tried to get Aly booted off the boat, and now Aly was making more sacrifices than the rest of them.

Her eyes fell on the Walkman still hanging over Aly's shoulder. She brightened when she saw that the battery door was open, and empty.

"Did you—"

Aly shook her head. "I couldn't get that close to him, and I didn't know where the batteries went inside him. But I managed to throw them into the backpack along with the other batteries."

Well, that was something. Eventually, Sebastien would be putting some used batteries into himself. But that could take weeks, months. And who knew if he would put them both in at once. The organization could accomplish a lot in the meantime.

Aly's attention turned to the corner of the room. "What's *his* problem?" Andy Six was still curled up, looking kind of pathetic.

"He tried to take my chocolate bar and I fought him off," Amy told her.

"Good for you! It looks like he's reviving now."

Sure enough, Andy Six was coming out of his fetal position. He still seemed dazed, but he managed to get to his feet. Amy couldn't see any trace of the cut on his arm. Apparently, he'd regained enough of his genetic superpower to have the rapid healing capability.

Something else about him had changed too. He wandered over to where the other treated clones were still standing guard with their weapons.

"Guns are bad," he said. "They can hurt people."

"Yeah," Andy Eleven replied. "That's the point."

"But it's wrong," Six said.

Eleven looked at the gun in his own hand. "You mean I'm not holding it right?"

"I mean you shouldn't hurt people. It's wrong."

Eleven stared at Six in disbelief. Five, One, Aly, and Andy were all listening and watching with their mouths open.

"What's going on?" Five wondered aloud. "What happened to him?"

Amy felt a lightbulb go on in her brain. More than a lightbulb—an extravaganza of fireworks. "Lulu's necklace," she breathed.

Andy gasped, and she could see that he understood. "The DNA from the stone age! There must be traces on the teeth. It counteracts the treatment and puts that gene back to sleep!"

Amy One's eyes widened. "You mean my Andy can be emotional again? Give me that necklace!"

But Amy had already figured out the possibilities. Quickly, she broke teeth off the leather thong and passed them to Aly, Andy, Five, and One. Together they attacked the other clones, who were so surprised, many of them dropped their guns. Others fired wildly into the air. Apparently no one had ever actually taught them how to use a gun. Andy and One jabbed the boys with the teeth, and One seemed to take particular pleasure in pricking Andy Eleven over and over. When Amy jabbed Aimee, the actress howled, but it wasn't from pain.

"That better not leave a scar!" she shrieked.

As each clone was jabbed with a tooth, he or she reacted just like Andy Six. They all whimpered and curled up on the floor. It wouldn't be long before their emotions returned. Each of them would have a conscience, something that would stop them from collaborating with the organization.

But the noise and the gunfire had drawn others to the room. Heavily armed, Sebastien and Annie burst in the room. No Stone Age horse tooth, Amy knew, would have the least effect on them.

fourteen

While Annie gathered the fallen guns, Sebastien surveyed the scene. There were clones curled up on the floor. Others were getting up, with dazed expressions. Amy One and Andy Eleven were already locked in an embrace.

Apparently, the human part of Sebastien could still feel emotions, and he was looking distinctly unhappy. He snatched a horse tooth from Aly's hand. "What ees zees?"

No one answered. The man who might or might not be Mr. Devon came in, and Sebastien showed him the tooth. "Do you know what zees ting ees?"

"No."

Amy's heart lifted. The real Mr. Devon had seen Lulu's necklace when Amy returned from the Stone Age. He knew exactly what it was. So this guy was either *not* the real Mr. Devon, or he was the real Mr. Devon playing double agent. Or something like that. It was starting to get very confusing.

Annie gave this Devon a gun, and Sebastien gazed over the group. "Does not anyone wish to stay on our side? To become a part of zee new world order?"

No one answered him.

Sebastien directed his eyes at Aimee. "Not even you? I could make you a star in Hollywood, you know."

"Really?" Aimee asked, but Five pinched her, hard. "Ow!"

A creepy smile came over Sebastien's face. "Well, it does not really matter what you want. You are staying right here while I have zees ting analyzed. It will be simple to discover what has interfered wiz our treatment. And even more simple to find a way to . . ." He paused for a second, as if searching for the right word. "To reverse it."

Amy looked at him sharply. Had Sebastien just faltered? Was he slowing down? Or was that just wishful thinking?

"I go now," he said. But he didn't get far. Two new figures appeared at the door. Another man who might or might not be the real Mr. Devon. And—

"Eve!" Amy cried out.

At the very same moment, Andy cried out, "Mom!"

Amy turned to him in disbelief. "What did you call her?"

It was Five who took advantage of the disruption. With a swift judo kick she knocked the gun out of Annie's hand. Andy and three other recovered clones jumped Mr. Devon.

"Give me a tooth!" Five yelled.

Amy wanted to tell her that it probably wouldn't do any good. Annie Perrault was just pure evil. She'd probably never been treated at all. She didn't need to lose her conscience—she'd never had one. But Amy tossed Five a tooth anyway, just for the pleasure of seeing Annie get jabbed again and again.

Andy was bent over his Devon, a huge tooth in his hand, and he was prepared to strike.

"No, don't!" the man yelled. "I'm the real Mr. Devon! I'm on your side!"

Amy ran to them. "He could be telling the truth, Andy."

"No, he's not." Those words came from the other Mr. Devon. "I'm the real Mr. Devon."

Andy hesitated. "I don't know who to believe!"

"Andy, *this* is Mr. Devon," Eve said, touching the arm of the man she was with.

"Are you *sure*, Mom?"

"Andy, why are you calling her Mom?" Amy cried out. "How could she be your mother? She's an accelerated Amy!"

There was anguish on Andy's face as he gazed deeply into Amy's eyes. "I wanted to tell you, in the right way. So it wouldn't come as such a shock."

"What are you talking about?"

"She's not an accelerated Amy," Andy said. "She's the *first* Amy. She's my mother, and . . . and in a way, she's your mother too." He looked around, and his gaze took in all the other Amys in the room. "She's the genetic basis of all of you."

Amy thought she'd stopped breathing. The room was spinning and her body was trembling. Eve was watching them nervously, her expression hopeful but fearful at the same time. When she spoke, her voice shook.

"I'm sorry I had to pretend to have lost my memory with some of you. It was the only way I could keep you from asking questions. When Mr. Devon told me he was coming back to this island, I told him I wanted to help save you. Because in a way, I'm responsible for the terrible situation you're in. You've all got other mothers, mothers who are more real to you than I am. I don't expect you to love me as you love them. But you're still a part of me. You *came* from me. And I love you, all of you."

Andy Eleven looked confused. "But . . . if you're Andy Five's mother, are you the mother of all the Andys?"

"No," Eve said. "Andy is my adopted son. I met Dr. Jaleski when he had just finished part one of Project Crescent. For part two, Dr. Jaleski used my genetic material to develop the Amy clones."

Andy looked at the face of the man he was still holding down. "Then who's this guy? I mean, he's clearly not a clone, and not an android. And he's not Mr. Devon."

"No, he's none of those things," Mr. Devon said. He went closer and looked at his twin on the floor. "Tell them who you are."

"Sebastien, what should I do?" the man cried.

It dawned on Amy that Sebastien hadn't said a word or moved in several minutes. He was still there, in the same upright position by the door. Was he actually giving up? Was he thinking that he'd been overcome?

As it turned out, Sebastien wasn't thinking anything at all. One of the Andys poked him . . . and he toppled over.

"He used the battery from your Walkman, Amy!" Aly yelled excitedly. "He's dead!"

"He is not dead!" This came from Annie Perrault, who'd been jabbed with a horse tooth a number of times. As Amy had suspected, it had had no effect on her. "Batteries can be replaced."

"Not when there isn't a case to hold it," Mr. Devon said. "There has to be a garbage incinerator around here somewhere."

This made Annie shriek. Breaking free from Amy Five, she ran at top speed from the building. An Andy and an Amy started after her, but Mr. Devon stopped them.

"Don't bother," he said. "She can't do any harm. The organization still hasn't worked out all the acceleration kinks. We won't have to worry about Annie Perrault much longer."

His replica on the ground was alarmed. "What do you mean? Is this acceleration going to kill us?"

"I'm not sure," Mr. Devon said. "All I know is that your body can't keep up with the genetic speed. Something has to give out."

"Wait a minute," Andy said. He looked at the man. "Are you saying that *you've* been accelerated?"

"Tell them," Mr. Devon said. "Tell them your name. It's time they all knew."

The man on the floor swallowed nervously. "I'm Andy Three. I'm one of you guys. Only accelerated."

"And you look just like Mr. Devon," Andy said. "Which means . . ."

Mr. Devon nodded. "I was the genetic basis in part one of Project Crescent."

Another Andy spoke. "Then you're our . . . our . . . father?"

"In a way."

Amy thought she'd have to pinch herself to keep from fainting. It was all falling into place, all the mysteries and secrets that had been a part of her life. All the bits and pieces . . . It was like a giant jigsaw puzzle had been finally completed . . . but what kind of picture did it produce?

She looked at Andy. He was clearly in a state of shock, staring at Mr. Devon, then at Eve, then back at Mr. Devon. It was as if he didn't know where to look, what to think, or how to make sense of it all.

Amy knew exactly how he felt.

fifteen

Nancy Candler moved through the living room, placing trays of snacks here and there. She was smiling and greeting people, and every time she passed Amy, she stopped and hugged her. Amy hugged back, harder than usual. She knew this couldn't be easy for Nancy—preparing to meet the woman who'd provided the DNA material to make her daughter. It wasn't going to be easy for Amy, either.

But there were friends around—Tasha, Eric, Chris—to lend support. Dr. Dave Hopkins had come too, and so had Andy.

"So all the clones are going to be okay, right?" Tasha asked.

Amy nodded. "Lulu's necklace got them feeling and caring again. And Andy Three's going to be all right, isn't he, Dr. Dave?"

The doctor nodded. "We're treating him with laser therapy. Slowly, of course, so we can control the deceleration process. I don't want him slipping back to infancy. He seems to be losing a year about every week, so he should be out of the hospital in three months."

Amy made a mental note to make herself available to him in case he wanted to talk. She knew what it felt like to go from being an adult to being a kid again.

"What about the organization?" Eric asked.

"I think the Washington headquarters has been closed down," Chris said. "I tried the phone number yesterday and got a recording saying it had been disconnected."

"Which doesn't mean they no longer exist," Andy said. "They could be setting up shop somewhere else. But I think Sebastien was the glue that held the group together. Without him, it will be a long time before they become active again."

"*If* they become active," Amy's mother said. "They may just give up."

But Dr. Dave agreed with Andy. "I don't think so, Nancy. As long as science holds the promise of changing the world, there will be people who will want to change it to their advantage. People who want to control nature, and not let it take its course."

"Isn't that what science and medicine is all about?" Amy pondered aloud. "I mean, if there were no experiments, we wouldn't have cures for terrible diseases, would we? Nature didn't provide the cures, science did."

Tasha nodded. "If we just let nature take its course, people would suffer."

"You're right," Nancy said. "Science is not the enemy. The problem comes when science is separated from ethics."

Amy thought about this. "What Dr. Jaleski did, cloning us and altering our genes . . . was that unethical?"

Nancy looked at Dr. Dave. "Who knows?" Dr. Dave said. "He certainly meant well. He wanted to spare people the heartache of genetic disease. But controlling what a human being has the capability to be, well, that can get dangerous."

"On the other hand," Nancy said, "where do you draw the line? A family requests genetic testing so their future child will not have a hereditary vision disorder. Another family wants to ensure that their child has blue eyes."

"Remember that awful boy genius, Adrian?" Tasha asked Amy. "He was using genetic experiments so people could create the kind of baby they wanted. That's got to be wrong."

It was all so complicated, and too much to contemplate. Besides, there was a more immediate concern now ringing the doorbell.

Amy opened the door. "Hello, Eve."

The woman smiled. "Hello, Amy."

Amy stepped aside to let her enter. A silence came over the room as Eve and Nancy Candler came face to face. Then Nancy opened her arms.

"Thank you," she said. "For giving me my daughter." The women embraced, and Amy relaxed. She would only have one mother—Nancy. But Eve would be a part of her life in some special way. Just like she'd become a part of the lives of all the Amys who wanted to know her.

Andy hugged his mother too, and said he had an announcement to make. "Mom's moving here to Los Angeles," he told the group. "I'm going to live with her. Chris too."

"That's wonderful!" Amy said. She looked at her mother anxiously to see how she was taking the news. But Nancy Candler seemed happy.

"It's been hard for us, not having more people we can share our secret with," she said. "I feel like our family is getting bigger. And I like it." She looked out the window. "Here comes another member of the family."

"Mr. Devon?" Amy asked.

"Yes. And he's got someone with him. I don't think I know her."

But Amy did. "Five," she said when the two visitors came in. "Hi."

"Hi, Seven. I hope you don't mind that I tagged along. I asked Mr. Devon to bring me."

"Five says you're the one she feels most like a sister to," Mr. Devon said. "Because you're so much alike."

It was true, Amy had to admit that. And it wasn't just their genes and their physical appearance.

Mr. Devon brought them up to date. The organization *had* closed down the Washington headquarters, and the group wouldn't be reestablishing itself anytime soon.

"They're on a government list," he told them. "They'll be watched very carefully."

"What about Annie Perrault?"

Mr. Devon shook his head. "No news there. She escaped. She may have gone back to France."

Amy wondered about certain others associated with the organization. "How about the pink-smocked girls? What's going to happen to them?"

"Oh, they'll be fine," Mr. Devon assured her. "They're going into a training program."

"What will they be trained to do?"

"They're going to be fashion models. They barely eat anything, so they're sure to stay skinny."

"And they're expressionless," Amy said. "That's perfect!"

"Have you heard from Aly?" Five asked Amy.

Amy nodded. "She's fine. You were right about her—she really came through for us. That dead battery exchange idea was very cool."

Five agreed. "But there's something I don't understand. Aly didn't actually get the batteries into Sebastien, just into his storage unit. Kind of a big coincidence that he just happened to pick your dead batteries to recharge himself."

"I was wondering about that too," Amy said. "But then I saw his regular batteries, the ones Aimee brought him. They were a cheap variety, the kind with no name. *My* batteries are advertised on TV with the wind-up bunny that keeps going. Sebastien must have thought they were better and decided to try them."

"That still doesn't make sense," Five said. "Couldn't he tell right off that they were dead? The Devon androids always knew when their batteries were running low."

The real Mr. Devon had an answer for her. "There was a difference between Sebastien and the androids. Sebastien had a human brain. In a way, he was too smart for his own good. With all the evil plans he had brewing, he didn't pay attention to the signals from his body."

Everything seemed to have come together. Amy gazed at her mother in wonderment. "It's over," she said. "All the fear, and the hiding, and the danger . . . it's over. I can be a normal person, I can live a normal life. So can Andy, and Five, and all of us."

Her mother smiled, but there was a hint of sadness in her eyes. "You'll never be completely normal, Amy. You do realize that."

"I know," Amy said.

"We all know that," Andy said.

"*I'm* going to be normal," Five said suddenly.

Amy turned to her. "What do you mean?"

Five pulled a lock of hair behind an ear and revealed small silver studs. "I've had my ears pierced."

Amy was shocked. "But—why?"

"Because I want to be really normal," Five said. "I don't want special powers and skills. I don't want to be stronger and smarter and faster than everyone else."

Amy couldn't believe this. She'd thought Five was so competitive. "But you're a born leader," she said.

Five nodded. "I am. So maybe I'll go into politics or something like that. But I want to do it naturally."

Amy remembered how she had felt when her own ears were pierced and she'd lost all her powers. She hadn't felt normal. She'd felt like half a person. So maybe she didn't really want to live a normal, ordinary life after all?

But later that evening, after everyone had gone home, she stretched out on the sofa in front of the TV and felt wonderful being safe and secure. Her mother was in the kitchen, fixing them dinners on trays so they could watch a good movie that was coming on in a few minutes. The next day, Amy was going to catch up on e-mails and invite Aly to come visit soon. Then she and Tasha would go to the mall and try on clothes. They would go to the movies with Andy and Chris. She'd be spending the weekend like any normal, ordinary, happy teenager.

She picked up the remote and clicked on the TV.

There was still a minute or two before the movie, and the news was on.

"Finally, we want to report on a bizarre and frightening occurrence in Paris, France, last night. During a ballet performance, a new member of a dance troupe began performing pirouettes along with the others onstage. But when everyone else stopped, she continued to spin. It is unclear if she couldn't or simply wouldn't stop. Her spinning accelerated to a speed that didn't seem humanly possible. Ultimately, her body gave out, and she collapsed onstage. Autopsy reports do not indicate the presence of any drugs, and the cause of this strange death remains a mystery."

But not to Amy.

Don't miss
the last book in the series

#24

Amy, on Her Own

Something is happening to Amy. It begins with the fading of the crescent moon mark on her shoulder. And as reports trickle in from sister clones who are encountering their share of sudden physical problems, Amy realizes that none of this bodes well.

How can the Amys be developing genetic abnormalities?

How can they be losing their extraordinary powers?

How can the deterioration be stopped?

Amy is stumped by the questions racing through her head. For so long, she has wanted to be "normal"—but that was before she risked losing everything that makes her special. . . .